I hate I
but I ...
you don't! ♥

C. McDonald
x

Capture Me

CHELSEA McDONALD

"Everyone looks bored here,
But I can't go home
So, I hide in the corner
Where the loners go
Put a drink to my lips
'Till the music's good
And I can't find your eyes yet
But I wish I could"
- Wait Up, Charlotte Lawrence

PROLOGUE
Ellie

I TURN TO WALK AWAY. I can't stand there any longer. I can still feel the heat of Michael's stare on my back as I move further and further away. It's only a ten-minute walk home but I already know it's going to be the longest, most excruciating ten minutes of my life. I hadn't chosen this spot on purpose, it's just lucky that it's close to home. When Michael picked me up for our date tonight I hadn't known this would be how the night would go. I'd been waiting for weeks for the timing to be right, tonight it had just felt right.

I could feel it as we drove to the cinema, the tension in the car. All throughout the film, I felt sick to my stomach, to the point where I actually wanted the sinking feeling to swallow me whole. I suffered through three hours of nerves before Michael drove me to our spot.

'Our spot' I focus on those two words. This won't be

our spot anymore. I probably won't ever be able to come here again without the memories of the heartbroken look on Michael's face, or of the pain that's pounding through my heart.

With the days whizzing by, the countdown was on. It was like there was this massive timer hanging above our heads. Or at least, hanging above mine. I don't know how Michael felt, or how he thought this would play out, but he must have known that something was wrong. As much as I didn't want my already made decision to affect the remaining time I had left with my long term high school sweetheart, it has been so hard trying to keep up the facade all this time.

This summer has been the worst, even worse than when my dad walked out on my family. I thought I'd never heal from that pain, that pain of not being wanted by a parent was the worst thing I would ever have to experience.

I was so wrong.

I take it slowly, one step at a time. I knew this was coming, I thought I had prepared myself for it well. Michael's glistening eyes flash inside my head, I immediately want to turn back and run into his arms.

As much as my heart is breaking I have to be strong. One of us has to. With him going off to college so far away, I can't be the one to hold him back from living his life to the fullest. I never thought I would be able to do this, I love Michael with all of my being. I thought he was it for me, my one true forever. I still feel that way now which makes this all that much harder.

Usually, when couples break up it's because of a

valid reason; he cheated on her, she is in love with someone else, or simply they've fallen out of love. This isn't the case for us, not at all. When Michael got accepted to Princeton, his dream school, we were over the moon. I was so happy for him; it was what he'd worked so damn hard for.

The questioning voice in the back of my head started to get louder and louder as the time for him to leave grew closer. We'd talked so much about what was going to happen to our relationship, Michael had been dead set on continuing our relationship long distance. I had loved the idea at first but the more I thought about it, the more I realized I'd be holding him back - keeping him tied down.

I continue down the brick-lined path, the trees and shrubbery start to hide me from Michael's line of sight. I want to look back, but with my face wet with tears I can't let him see how much this is killing me.

I just need to keep moving, to make it back home. Evan will most liking be waiting for me, as he has done for the past few weeks. I hadn't needed to say anything, but he knows. Maybe it's a twin thing, but he does seem to know me better than I know myself.

CHAPTER ONE

Ellie

THIS IS BULLSHIT!

I need new friends, badly. I take another look around me and start feeling the desperation kick in. Of course, these lot aren't my only friends. I have friends from work and even a couple from high school. But none of whom I'm close enough to, to be able to call up and arrange to meet them for coffee.

It's always just been me and Evan. I've never had many friends because I've never really needed any. I had my brother and he was all I needed. But now, as an adult, it's different - it's not us against the world anymore. Don't get me wrong, we're still super close, just not as close as we once were.

As with everything in life, nothing lasts forever. And with that, unfortunately, there's no one else that I'd want to be spending my birthday with, no matter how shitty my current company is being.

And the reason for my pissed off attitude? Today is my birthday. Well mine and Evan's birthday, and we've come out to celebrate with our group of friends. It's not the fact that I have to share the birthday spotlight with my twin, it's not the fact that we're out at Lane's bar - yet again. I love being out, no matter where we are, and cocktails are definitely the best when they're made by one of Lane's bartenders.

No. The fact that all seven of us are sitting in our regular booth and I'm the most single person here, that's what's really pissing me off.

It's pissing me off so much that even Lane's cocktails aren't working their regular magic.

Normally this kind of thing doesn't get to me that much. I consider myself the laid-back one of the group but lately it's been more and more evident that this is now a couples group. First, there was Gabby, then Luke and Tash and now my brother. Although Evan and Kate aren't officially a couple, yet, they may as well be. They're either at each other's throats or they're *at each other's throats* - if you know what I mean.

It gets boring being left on my own while they're all pairing off. It makes me think that maybe I'm the weird one because I'm not in a relationship. But I'm not looking for a relationship right now, all guys are stupid and I don't want any part of that.

My friends laugh when I say that, but they're not the only ones. Everyone seems to have a reaction when I spend half an hour trying to convince them that boys are icky. I can quite easily admit that yes I do sound like a child, but I really couldn't care less. Little girls have the right freaking idea on that one!

I strongly believe in the opinion that guys don't mature as fast as girls, and that's why it'd be pointless trying to date someone now. I could always date older but that idea just doesn't quite appeal to me as much as being single does. I like my freedom, and not having to check in with someone all the time. And I absolutely love that I don't have to pretend to give a shit about how someone else's day at the office went.

My mother says that makes me selfish but I've been called worse by dates, so the insults tend to bounce right off my skin by now. I like to do me, whatever that may mean.

My brother and Luke finally detached from the group to grab another round of drinks from the bar. I dive back into conversation hoping it might be something more stimulating with just the girls, plus Sam.

I listen for a minute. Nope, apparently not.

"Do you know what color dress you're going for?"

"I'm thinking the traditional white but Sam's mom is trying to convince me to wear the dress she wore. She's been so helpful that I don't know what to say."

"Well, do you want to wear her dress? At the end of the day, it's your wedding and you need to be happy with what you decide." Tash blinks those big doe-like eyes at Gabby as she speaks from the heart.

How many drinks has she had?

I don't know Tash as well as I know Gabs and Katie

but I've never seen her quite so calm. Quiet, yes but that's a totally different thing to calm in my book.

"Yeah, I know. And truth be told, I haven't even seen it yet. I'm thinking maybe just wait until I've seen it to make up my mind." Gabby finally smiles, I see Sam squeeze her hand. They share a loving look that's almost sickly sweet. My gut prickles with envy. I'm super happy for them, but that look just gets me every time. I think it's because I've had that, I've shared that look with someone before, and it sucks ass that I lost it.

"I'm sure it'll be gorgeous babe," Kate says around a mouthful of rum and coke, she slurps down the rest of her drink before continuing her sentence. "And if it's not, she'll understand if you tell her that you want to pick out your own dress. Hell, it's your big day, it's not like she's going to say 'no' to you."

I have to clench my teeth to swallow my yawn. Don't get me wrong, I'm ecstatic from Sam and Gabby. They're so happy together, and I wish them all the happiness in the world. But, at the same time, with me being the resident commitment-phobe I'm so not interested in all the wedding stuff. I was actually shocked at how much planning, and fucking money, went into a wedding.

I don't see myself as an attention hog, but is it too much to ask to just hang out with my friends on my birthday? No wedding stuff, no mushy crap. Just the seven of us hanging out as *friends*.

Well, apparently, it is too much to ask. I watch on as Katie continues downing her shots like the glasses are filled with apple juice and not tequila. She's definitely gonna be bent over the rim of a toilet in an hour or two.

I chew on my straw getting more annoyed by the second that I'm the party pooper tonight. Not that anyone's noticed but I switched to diet coke two drinks ago. With the way the others are going I'm guessing no one volunteered to be the designated driver for tonight, they'll probably split a cab. Or I'll end up driving the fuckers home - which is most likely. I sink further into my seat, my party mood has now completely left the station, so I may as well get comfortable. At least the music is good and my phone is fully charged. It's barely midnight yet, tonight's going to be a long one.

CHAPTER TWO

HER SMILE IS LUMINOUS; it expels energy into the world all around her. My heart aches as her smile widens. She's beautiful and radiant as always, but she's different now - free, almost as if she's untouchable.

Fuck! My mind starts to scramble; my mouth is at a total loss for words.

I quickly turn on my heel and rush to exit the bar before she spots me - it wouldn't be hard. I'm naturally quite tall anyway but if that doesn't put a spotlight on me, the fact that I'm standing and staring open-mouthed at her, that would sure do it.

I pull out my phone and shoot a text to my friends. I've only been back in town a couple of days, I'm sure they'll be able to wait another day for our long-awaited boy's night.

I must admit I don't come back to town as much as I should, more often than not I'll fly momma out to see me instead. She's never once complained but I think that's because she knows, even after all this time, it's still too painful for me to come back here.

I hate that. I loathe it entirely. The fact that I can't come back to a town I grew up in because I got my heart broken when I was in high school - it's downright pathetic.

She may have been, in my mind, 'the one' but that doesn't excuse the fact that I should've moved on by *now* - years after the fact.

Another very small reason I don't like to visit, my hatred - for her and for myself. The woman who walked away, so easily leaving me behind, broken and battered. It's also where my self-hatred stems from, the fact that I let her make me feel that way. She made me feel so weak and helpless, I hated how little control I had over that situation.

From that day forward I knew I'd never let anyone have that control over me again. I remember in high school, I had thought all those guys that slept around had no idea what they were missing. Turns out I maybe should've been paying more attention, because as I watched Ellie walk out of my life forever I was thinking maybe they did know what they were missing.

I lean against the car and breathe a deep breath trying to clear the haze that I've somehow gotten myself lost in. This is what she does to me, she makes me crazy. The fact that I want to both run to her and run from her is the definition of insanity in my book.

I finish typing out the text to Davey and Simon. I ask if we can meet tomorrow for lunch instead. Simon replies more or less straight away, easily agreeing to the change of plans. I'm staying with Lynch so I'll just talk to him about the change of plans when I get back to the house.

It's not until I'm exiting the messages app on my phone that the date on the calendar catches my attention. *Shit!*

No wonder she's out having a good time, it's her and Evan's birthday. If I had have known that beforehand, I wouldn't have bothered to make plans for tonight.

The sudden realization has me feeling like a major dick. If Ellie is here celebrating her birthday I have no doubt that Evan is close by celebrating as well. Those two were always oddly close, even for twins, but I'd always gotten along with Ellie's family - especially her twin brother Evan. If it had been him I'd seen, it would've been a different story, I would've gone up to him to wish him a happy birthday. I might've even tried to strike up a conversation like I would with an old buddy. As far as I'm concerned there's no bad beef between Evan and me.

CHAPTER THREE

Ellie

I GROWL ONCE AGAIN, making sure to stamp my feet extra hard on the hardwood floors. My aim is to ruin Evan's slumber and annoy him until he's on my level of pissed. From the amount he drank last night I'm guessing he'll already have a pounding headache when he wakes up. *Good*. The jerk totally deserves it. It may be childish, but right now, it's the only thing that's making me feel any better about last night.

Not only had everyone partnered off, leaving me to not only sit but dance on my own as well. But then they all got butt-fuck wasted, and I was left as the responsible one. Me? Anyone who ever thinks that is a good idea definitely doesn't know me that well. I can barely keep all my fish alive, I am not up to the standard of looking after live people!

I did it anyway, mainly because I couldn't leave my brother out to dry. My mother would go ballistic on my ass. I've always had a sneaking suspicion that Evan's always been her favorite child, if anything were to happen to him she'd know it was my fault somehow.

I got used to her favoritism over time, I tried not to let it bother me because I knew she wasn't doing it on purpose. I don't even think she realized she was doing it. But it was mainly little things that would tip me off, like when we were in school, and we were ill. Mom would always say I was faking it, so she'd send me on my way to school, but Evan? Not once in our lives has mom called him out on his bullshit. And I know exactly how many times he played the 'sick' card too! He hated his geology teacher, and he had her every Tuesday and Thursday.

A loud snore shakes the kitchen walls pulling me from my inner thoughts. Damn brother sleeps like he's fucking dead, except for all the noise. Poor Katie.

Luckily all of our friends live relatively close by so it wasn't a massive feat dragging their asses home. It honestly took more effort trying to smush them all in my car. I made it work eventually - with a lot of tangled limbs, groans of drunken annoyance and almost some slammed-in-the-car-door fingers.

That last one may or may not have been accidentally on purpose. It was a long hellish night! If you've ever been the designated driver then that's how shitty I felt by the end of the night, or worse. And, on top of all that, when I woke up this morning I realized that my purse is missing. Best guess is I left it at Lane's last night, or more like, my only guess because we didn't go anywhere else.

Grrrrrrr!

It didn't have much cash in, thankfully by that point of the night, I would've spent most of what I took out with me. It had a few credit cards, all of which I froze the second I found out they were missing, and a tube of my favorite lipstick. Overall, I'm more pissed because it was my favorite purse! I only have the one and that means if I can't find it I'm going to have to spend the rest of the day at the shops, trying to find another one that I don't find ugly or ridiculous.

I slam the door behind me, my car keys jingling in my hand as I leave the house and head for the bar. Logically, that's the only place I could've left it. Of course, I know it's wishful thinking that someone hasn't already picked it up but I cross my fingers and pray for it to still be there.

It's lunchtime and while the row of shops and cafes are bouncing with people, the bar looks dead. If I didn't know any better, I'd say it was closed. I push through the door and examine the bar, Lane is at the far end wiping down the bar. I make a beeline over to him; I figure it'll be easier to check if anything's been handed in before I start searching the bar on my hands and knees.

He sees me rushing in and smiles. I've known him a while but only because he serves us the best cocktails in town, they have me coming back quite regularly. "Hey Lane, you know if anything was handed in last night?"

He raises an eyebrow, "Let me check."

I drum my fingers against the wooden topped bar,

Lane drops down beneath the bar. When he speaks, his voice is muffled, "What is it that you've lost?"

"My purse. It's pink, it's got a glittery pattern on one side of it. Well, you'll know if you take a look inside of it, it has my driver's license and all of my bank cards. Or, at least I'm hoping it does," I huff. It better still have my new credit card - I only got it the other day. I haven't even had a chance to break it in yet.

"This it?" One arm pops up into view, clutched in its grip is my purse - or it looks like it as far as I can tell.

"Think so," I pluck it from Lane's hand as he stands back up. I tug at the zipper to check its contents. Driver's license, credit cards, cash - check. The only thing I spot that's missing is, oh wow. "The fuckers stole my condom," I gasp.

Lane starts cracking up and even I've got to admit that's pretty funny, "Serves them right, it's been in there a decade. Hope it broke on them," I exclaim. "It's okay, it's not like I was actually ever going to use it."

I've only ever slept with one person, someone I loved and trusted. But even after that fiasco, I wouldn't even feel safe having sex with him. Not that there's any chance of that. If the condoms didn't work with him there's no one else I'm willing to fucking try them with.

The girls don't know that it's been eight years since I've had sex. But, they also don't know that I know what it's like when you accidentally get knocked up. I don't know that I could ever take that risk again. Only one person has ever made me feel that way, wild and free - throwing all caution to the wind.

Think of the devil and he may appear. Because, holy-fucking-shit, there he is.

It's possible that I've been abducted, drugged and then returned to Lane's, isn't it? I feel like that's the only possible explanation for what's happening right now. Because surely I'm not actually seeing the man that I loved and set free eight years ago, and haven't seen since, standing less than ten feet away.

Or maybe, I'm just a fucking magician. The first thought I've had of Michael in at least a month and poof there he is. He's beautiful, even more so than I remember. Michael had always been so striking, the exact definition of tall, dark and handsome. But with the bluest blue eyes.

"Michael?" I can't help but question - stupidly. He's grown out the scruff on his face and he's dressed impeccably, but I know it's him.

I can't place the look that takes over his face when he sees me for the first time. I think it might be confusion, but I've got to be honest, if he's confused about who I am I may just go ape shit. "It's Ellie? From high school?"

Oh, you know. Just the girl that you were madly in love with, that got pregnant and then broke your heart only weeks before you left for college. I mean it may have been eight years ago but it hasn't been long enough to forget the first girl who dumped you.

His laugh lines show when he smiles, it's somewhat tight-lipped like he doesn't want to laugh but my idiocy has forced him into it. "I know who you are."

Well, thank fuck for that! A small victory for today.

"Oh," I wanna ask why he didn't fucking say so but I zip my lip. "So, you're back in town?"

I haven't seen him in person since I broke up with him, the summer before I started my senior year. The last I heard about Michael, he was across the country busting the balls of a hacker. But even that was at least a year ago now that I think about it. I even remember crying when I read the news article - it was a proper Ben & Jerry's Cookie Dough kind of cry too.

"I'm actually on vacation at the minute. Mom keeps saying that I need to visit more often." He shrugs his shoulders with a wistful smile on his face.

Or at all. As far as I know, this is the first time he's come back to little old Aurora. Once he left for Princeton he's never looked back.

My god, he looks good though. He's always been gorgeous but it's definitely more of a rugged gorgeousness now. He's taller, he's got a hint of a five o'clock shadow, and his shoulders seem broader - like way more sculpted than before. I think it's the first time I've ever really understood that saying 'you've grown into yourself'.

The pain and regret over breaking up with him never really went away, even after all these years. But in the end, it had been my decision and that means I'm not allowed to be sour about the love of my life moving on with his life.

"It's been so long... I'm glad I got the chance to run into you." I smile as widely as I can without pulling a facial muscle. I take a step back needing to retreat, "Maybe I'll see you around."

God, I hope not.

I don't hang around any longer, I physically can't. At any moment, I'm going to burn up in flames, or burst out crying. And not the pretty crying where you shed a tear or two. The loud, sobbing, my-mouth-won't-close type of crying.

I don't even make it out the door of the bar when I start to feel my eyes misting up. I quickly swipe at my eyes and rush to my car. The weather is surprisingly warm, any other day I'd be out with my friends soaking up the sun and all its warmth. I usually welcome the warm weather, it's like a big comforting hug, but today is unlike any other day. The weather feels like it's against me, the heat suffocating me and constricting my dry throat.

Stop being a baby! I feel like slapping myself for letting my emotions take a hold of me. Running into Michael like that was not how I'd thought my day would go. It was a major shock to the system but I'm sure that in a few days I'll be as right as rain. I trick myself into believing that, just for now. I need to get home; only there will I be allowed to properly wallow in self-pity.

Michael had been a big part of my life once upon a time, and letting him go was the second hardest thing I've ever had to do. But, more than anything I know it was the right thing to do.

When I get home, I grab the tub of Ben & Jerry's that I have stashed in the freezer, for emergencies only, then I lock myself in my bedroom. I blast the television so that Evan won't be able to hear me, change my clothes and then do what I always do when I get a bit sentimental. I pull out my high school photo album.

It's not really a high school photo album, the only photos in it are of Michael and me - we just happened to be in high school at the time. But it's the only memento I let myself keep from that relationship.

I flip through the pages, I'm only torturing myself but I like the ache that throbs in my chest. That ache makes me feel alive, it reminds me that what I felt wasn't all in my head. A very real pain for a very real love that I'd once felt.

CHAPTER FOUR

HOLY FUCK. Okay, what the hell was that?

I'm frozen in place - I probably look like a real idiot. But I find myself caught between wanting to run after her and wanting to return to my friends with my head held high.

What would I even say to her if I did catch up to her? I don't know. All these years I thought the next time I saw her I wouldn't have anything to say. The truth is I feel the opposite, there's so much to say that I can't seem to form a complete sentence.

One thing that is at the forefront of my mind; that was definitely not how that was supposed to go down. I haven't seen Ellie, my high school sweetheart, in years. The day we broke up, the day she threw my heart away without glancing back, was most definitely the last time I'd seen her. I've spent all this time building up a scenario of how our first run-in would go, fretting over how I'd react in the moment. When she hadn't even given me time to react.

She looked so sad, almost haunted - nothing like the girl I saw last night. I hate to admit how much it tears me apart to see her miserable. It's wrong.

I've spent so much time being miserable, all because of her. It's wrong for me to feel sorry for her, I shouldn't feel anything for her. I should be over her and everything that happened between us all those years ago.

I rejoin my friends but I think even they can tell that my heart's not here, and my mind certainly fucking isn't. They both went AWOL as soon as Ellie ran out those doors.

I down the rest of my drink but don't order another one, I don't think I could compel myself to stay even if I did want to.

"So...?" After a beat of silence, I look up. Simon's looking at me expectantly, clearly that question had been aimed at me.

I rub a hand over my face hoping it will somehow, magically clear my head. I turn my attention solely to Simon, determined to hear him this time. "I'm sorry, what?" I question him.

He laughs, "I said, you'll be here Friday night, right?"

"Oh, yeah. I don't know how long I'm here for yet, but it will be until Monday at the earliest," I tell him.

"Well, then you'll have to come along to the bachelor party. It's gonna be an epic night. Gotta do it right, send our groom off in style." Davey claps Simon on the shoulder. I pretend not to see the way Simon's face tints pink. It makes me wonder what they're doing to 'send him off in style'. Whatever it is, I highly suspect that's why Simon's anxious. Hell, knowing Davey as well as I do, I'd be anxious too. The guy is a total wild card.

Davey continues ribbing Simon about his upcoming nuptials. I wrap it up with the guys fairly soon after that, that run-in with El still plays on my mind. I know she won't be coming back anytime soon but I'm rocked to my very core. The guys only let me leave after I finally agree to come out on Friday for Simon's bachelor party. It'll be horrible and will definitely include strippers of some sort, if for no one else's pleasure other than Davey's. But that's okay, he can have my share.

Outside the bar, I head to my car. I drove it here all the way from New Haven which is why when I look at my nice new car it's covered in shit. My Challenger is barely recognizable. I jump in and make the short drive over to momma's house.

When the two-story ranch type house comes into view it's like breathing in fresh air. This house was home to me for so long that it's like seeing an old relative. I've been in town a few days now but the effects still haven't worn off yet.

"Momma?" I call, my voice ringing throughout the house louder than I had intended.

"In here."

I follow the sound of her voice to the kitchen. "Hey, momma." I plant a kiss to her cheek before quickly moving out of her way. Her brown hair is tied up in a bun, she's armed with an apron and a whisk - she's clearly busy.

"What's all this?" I lift the lid on a pot that's on the stove. Peeking inside, I see shredded leaves of purple cabbage. I quickly replace the lid to shield it from my drooling. "It smells amazing."

"What are you talking about? I'm just preparing dinner," she simply says. I send a confused look to her back.

Did I miss half the day? My eyes flicker up to the clock hanging on the wall. Nope, it's still only two o'clock. Someone's eager for dinner.

"You feeling okay mom?"

"Of course, why do you ask?" She smiles sweetly as if this is all completely normal. Has she not noticed the state of the kitchen? It's a fuckin' mess. The benchtops are so completely filled that I have trouble remembering what color they were. And she must have every kitchen appliance she owns, out and on the go.

"No reason. It is just you and me for dinner tonight, isn't it?"

"Why yes, who else do you think I'd be inviting? Is there someone you wanted to bring along? I'm sure there's enough, I can always make more though."

"NO." I wince immediately at how loud I say it. "Sorry. I mean, this will be more than enough. I'm going to head back out, is there anything you needed?"

"Oh, yes! Could you please pick me up some more butter? The half a dish I have in the fridge won't last long once I get into it," she says.

"Sure, momma. I'll be back soon." I pick up my keys and wallet from the entry table before making my way to the car.

I'm almost to the grocery store when I spot it. The park. The amount of memories I have of that place almost can't be contained inside of me. Momma used to take me there as a child, she'd push me on the swings until the sun went down. Then in middle school, Davey and I used to play soccer on the field on Saturdays.

It was where I saw Ellie for the first time. Our first date, first kiss, happened right by the lake. Then the summer before I left for college, it was where Ellie let me go.

I pull into the parking lot of Walmart, slam the car into park and practically jump out of the car. Maybe this isn't such a good idea, after all.

I haven't even told mom yet, so realistically if I wanted to back out I easily could.

My visit back to Aurora, Illinois was not as innocent as I'd led everyone to believe. When momma broke her ankle, a fair few months ago now, I asked my boss if I could be transferred to an office closer to home. It was only a broken ankle but it scared me, because what if next time it's not just a broken ankle. I wasn't here to help her - to take care of her, I felt like the worst son.

A couple weeks ago when a position came up at Lisle, Illinois, I'd thought it was fate. Less than an hour away. But now, being here, I don't know if I could cope with all the memories I have here.

The main ones are the reminders everywhere of

Ellie. They hurt. It's why I've spent the last eight years of my life living anywhere but here - I was happy to.

My breath rushes from my lungs. I use the car as support to keep my body upright. *Have I just made the biggest mistake of my life?* I could always ask to get transferred back. I could move to Lisle, that would definitely limit my time driving back and forth around here.

Damn it! I feel myself tearing, being pulled in so many different directions. I'm in so many minds about what to do. I love Ellie, I hate Ellie. I wanna be near her but I know that I need to stay away. I need to protect my heart from her because I know that she's that only one that could so easily crush it, she's done it once before. What's to stop it from happening again?

I give myself a moment to clear all of my thoughts. It's difficult but I do it, push everything aside and right myself. As I enter the store I come to the decision that I may need someone else's opinion on this. I clearly can't be trusted to figure out my life on my own.

CHAPTER FIVE

Ellie

IT'S HIM. I know it, I can feel it in my gut. I hadn't necessarily been searching for him, but he has been weighing on my mind ever since we ran into each other. Or, at least, more than usual.

He hasn't seen me yet, his back is to me. I was driving past on the way home from work, albeit the long way home, but I wanted to chance a peek.

"Don't hate me. Please." I broach as I step closer, my voice quiet as not to startle him.

"El. You really shouldn't go sneaking up on people." His head turns, his face lifts to look at me.

'El' God, I love how he uses my old nickname. My mom calls me El, my brother on occasion - usually when he's drunk. But none of that could compare to the way his raspy voice speaks it. It sounds like it could be a different language, our own secret language.

"You may have been miles away but I've still been

able to feel it. I know you resent me but you need to know, now, that it was for the best." I take a seat on the grass a few feet away.

"In a way, I do. But that doesn't make me like it, it doesn't make that old ache hurt any less." His voice is gruff, on the edge of angry. I know he has a point, it doesn't help dull the pain just because you know it was the right decision. But to know that he still feels the pain too, it's grounding.

"I think, as hard as it is, we both need to move on. I know it would take time but I want your forgiveness."

He's silent for a long time. It puts me on edge to not know what he's thinking. "I don't hate you."

"What?" I ask.

"I like to think I do, it's supposed to make it easier. I hate what you did, but I could never hate you," he says quietly.

Good to hear because I still fucking love you.

"I couldn't look at you, I felt so broken inside. I was afraid if I saw the look on your face that I would crumble. Afterwards, I went home, I wouldn't leave the house until I knew that you'd left town for good," I tell him.

"So, how's life in the F.B.I?" I ask hoping to change the subject.

"It's different than what you think it's going to be. But I like the work, it keeps me busy," he says.

"And where are you based? Last I heard you were in L.A. that was a while ago now though," I say.

"That was a few years ago, I didn't like it much but I've been in Connecticut for over a year now. But I think that'll change soon though," he tells me mysteriously.

"Why's that? You getting itchy feet again?" I question.

He laughs, a proper throw your head back and have at it laugh. It makes me smile to see how relaxed he is now compared to a couple days ago. "I've just accepted a promotion. I requested to be moved to an office closer to home. They offered me a job on the Cyber Squad up here in Lisle," he tells me.

"But that, that's like... less than an hour away?" I stutter. Oh. Shit.

"Yeah, I know. I felt guilty when I couldn't be here for momma when she broke her ankle last year. I just thought it was time for a change. Time for me to finally come home and face my demons." He smiles.

"Well thank you very much but you know, I'd rather be called a witch over a demon. Makes me sound more feminine." I stretch my legs out and pose for effect.

It's supposed to be a joke but as his eyes do a long sweep of my figure I can see he clearly hasn't taken it that way. When his eyes lock on mine I'm all ready to set him straight, to throw a bucket of water on him. But then I see the heat in his eyes, it captures me locking me in its flame. It's been so long since I've felt his raw hunger for me, I've missed his touch, the way he can make my body flame and shiver at the same time.

When my eyes shift from his face I see that we're closer, only a foot of free space between us. I don't know who to thank for removing the space between us, me or him. His hand moves on top of my mine, it's the only thing that connects us. I look back up to see that he's leaning in closer. I don't want him to stop but he has to know before this goes any further, that this is not the reason I came here. "Michael."

"You know that I didn't come here for this, right?" My voice is all but a breathy whisper. My heart pounds against my ribcage and I worry I might pass out, or that Michael will hear it and think there's something medically wrong with me.

"I know." He's close enough now that I can feel his breath brush against my lips. I keep my eyes trained on his lips, soft and luscious - they look so inviting. I know what they taste like and I miss it, I crave it. I've been craving this for eight long years, for just another taste of him.

His lips finally press firmly against mine but immediately I know it's not enough. I need more. He's a drug and I'm his addict. I've been clean for eight years but it all comes flooding back, the rush of adrenaline from that first hit only makes you need it more.

My arms wrap around his neck not so innocently dragging my chest in until it's flush with his. My fingers rake through his soft brown hair taking their time and enjoying the sensations. Goosebumps begin to rise all over my body from the gentle caress of his hand on my thigh, he twiddles the material of my dress between his long fingers.

My tongue does a sweep of his mouth spurring his decision - his hand slides under the hemline of my skirt. His thumb grazes the edge of my panties, his fingers splayed over my hip.

A whistle breaks through my senses, our own little bubble suddenly broken. I pull my lips back from Michael's to look for the sound. My hackles start to relax when I spot the elderly man playing catch with his dog.

"We should get out of here." I rush out to Michael, my chest is heaving at the feel of Michael's lips continuing to run themselves over my neck and shoulder. He makes a rumble of agreement before we start to move towards the car park. Despite the interruption, the spell has somehow not been broken.

Hand in hand, I follow in Michael's hasty footsteps as we head for his car. It's less than a ten-minute drive to my house but it's most definitely going to be the longest ten minutes in history. Michael rounds the front of a fancy Dodge and opens the passenger side door for me. I slide in and watch as he's racing back around for the driver's door. He tosses out a quick 'buckle up' before revving the engine.

CHAPTER SIX

ELLIE JUMPS from the car before I even put it in park. I'm right behind her though. She throws open the door to her three-floor walkup and drags me inside. "Upstairs."

I dutifully follow her as she leads me up the stairs, past the living room and through to her bedroom. I shut the door behind me. I guessed from the shoes lying around and the framed football jersey on the wall in the living room, she either has a roommate or she shares the place with Evan. I'd bet on the latter and there is no way I want Evan to come barging in when I'm balls deep in his sister. That'd be awkward. For extra precaution, I check that the door is securely locked.

This is it. There's no turning back now. Before entering the bedroom I could've pulled back, said 'no' but now it's on. We're trapped and now there's nowhere else to run.

It's late afternoon but the daylight is still streaming in through the window. Ellie's across the room, she seems to have shied away. Me? I'm like a wild cat ready to pounce on my prey. But Ellie's always made me feel that way. It wasn't until the beginning of senior year that I started learning to control it, or maybe ignore it is a better description.

Running my eyes up and down the length of El's body I can feel myself lick my lips. That short, pathetic excuse of a dress hugs her figure, almost to the point that I never want her to wear it again. I picture her flouncing around in that dress for everyone to see and I need my hands on her.

Maybe this isn't a good idea. Nothing good ever comes from sexing up your ex, not to mention there will most definitely be the 'where's this going' speech afterwards. While my brain knows that this isn't a good idea that's not where my blood is flowing to, it's not in charge anymore. For the first time in eight years, my cock is in charge, he's the king and his word is the law. Just for tonight, I let my body take control, maybe one night is all it needs to convince my sound mind that this is worth the fallout that will fall - one way or the other.

I stalk forwards, not being able to stand the distance between us any longer. I intend to make her feel so good that she won't realize I've shredded her dress, making damn sure she never wears it in public again. As an F.B.I agent, you need to have a sense of control and discipline. As a career that may have been the best fit for me - I love my job. But when it comes to Ellie she's always been the only thing to ever push my boundaries, to test the limits of my control. Things have not changed, maybe they've even become worse. You know what they say, 'absence makes the heart grow fonder'.

No, Ellie seems to have only made my cock twice as hard and even more angry. He's ready to take back what's his, what he's been yearning for all these years.

I run my hands up Ellie's bare thighs before yanking the skirt up until it's snuggly settled around her waist. I strip off my jacket before sinking to my knees. My fingers begin to trace their own path up the back of her calves. Her knees buckle slightly as I pass over them but I continue up her thighs until her ass cheeks fill my palms.

The need to worship her continues to grow steadily, the scent of her arousal drives me into a frenzy. The evidence of how badly she wants this - wants me - pools only inches from my lips. That alone is enough temptation to tip any man over the brink of insanity.

Grabbing the sides of her panties, my eyes flickering up as I slowly begin peeling the pink lace from her body. Her eyes are closed, no objection on her face only the mask of anticipation. I continue sliding my hands down her legs until her panties are nothing but a puddle of wet lace on the floor.

Nudging her knee to spread her legs I move between them. Tilting my head my nose brushes against the soft patch of curls between her thighs. I

inhale the sweet scent of her arousal which only makes my already throbbing cock jerk against the constraint of my jeans. The first flicker of my tongue against her clit has El quivering above me. I quickly know that she won't last long like this, my sweet girl is on the edge.
 "When was the last time you came, Ellie?"

Her eyes fly open and watch as I drag my tongue through her puffy pink pussy lips, from her tight hole to her swollen nub. Her breath hitches when I wiggle the point of my tongue back and forth. "I ca-came last week," she stutters out.

"Was it your touch that made you come?" I tease her clit with a graze of my teeth. She cries out a 'yes', her eyes closing as I suck her clit into my mouth. I can tell she's close to orgasm when her hips start to buck against my face.

I run a finger around her tight opening, it's slick, a gentle push is all it takes to be knuckle-deep inside my favorite place to be. A slight curl of my finger and a gentle flick of my tongue is all it takes for my tightly wound El to come undone. Her body spasms, her lips breathing my name as her thighs try their hardest to clamp themselves shut. God, it's been so long since I've heard that hypnotic whisper.

I lap up all that she's willing to give me before I rise back to my feet. My hands immediately fly to the zip of my jeans. I free my cock, giving it a hard tug hoping to relieve some pressure.

Ellie recovers quickly, her big brown eyes flashing with excitement as she watching my cock bounce in my hand. I'm afraid I've just awoken the beast inside her.

I'm only just getting warmed up but it's an easy guess to say that it's going to be a long night. There's years and years of pent up sexual energy to be spent tonight, to finally be unleashed and I don't plan on letting go of her until I'm sated.

Up on her tippy toes, Ellie's mouth claims mine. Her arms wrapping around me, touching me, stroking me. She removes my t-shirt quickly, her nimble fingers going for my belt next. I help her in pushing down my jeans and boxer shorts. Next to go is Ellie's dress, I rip it from her body and toss it aside.

Both finally naked I back El up, the back of her legs hitting the bed frame, she lands on the bed with a soft bounce. Her hair fans out behind her, her arms by her sides, her perky little tits invite me to fondle them.

"Please Michael. Don't make me wait for it." She begs, her legs wrap around me, pulling me closer to where I need to be. Her knees fall wider enticing me to take full advantage of her position.

I don't need enticing though, I line myself up with her pussy sliding myself through her thick folds. "You want this? Sweetheart, I'm gonna give it to you."

With the extra lubrication from her juices, the beefy head of my cock nudges through her pussy with a slick pop. My cock isn't even fully saddled yet and her hips are rocking up to meet mine, she's thirsty for more. I go slow wondering how long I can draw this out before Ellie fucks herself using my dick. She throws her head back and groans, "Quit teasing."

My resolve snaps, I impale her. "Fuck."

"Yes," her voice whispers shakily.

I grip her hips and use all the momentum to draw out and slam into her repeatedly. This is rough fucking, it's purely for a carnal purpose. There'll be time for the sweet stuff later on.

With every thrust of my hips, Ellie's cries grow louder. The pressure begins building up, the walls of her pussy starting to tighten and spasm around me. In eight years, I've never felt so welcomed. This is exactly where I'm meant to be, this was what I was made for.

El's knees that are hooked around my hips squeeze me as her body starts to quake, her hips bolting off the bed. I collapse lightly on top of her to capture her lips in a searing kiss. It's barely enough to contain her pleasure as she climaxes around him. I've never been able to forget how vocal El is in bed, she's a screamer alright. It's one of the things that draws my balls tight and sink into my own orgasm.

With every pulsing clench of Ellie's pussy walls, she draws out my release. With everything spent I pull out and fall to the bed next to El. I try to calm my own breathing as she does the same. I'm covered in sweat, I feel like I've just run a marathon but the rhythmic sound of Ellie's panting is soothing. Almost hypnotic.

CHAPTER SEVEN

Ellie

MOVEMENT beside me starts to clear the sleep from my mind. I stretch out in bed to feel that I'm the beds only current occupier. My muscles are stiff, they've never been worked out that hard before. I feel a dull ache between my legs but it only makes me smile. We really went at it last night.

Round one was a hard quick fuck, but I didn't mind it. I loved it in fact but it didn't beat out rounds two, three, and four. They were sweet and tender filled with hot kisses and heart-warming words of worship. What can I say, we didn't want to waste any of the night away. I dozed off a few times only to wake up to Michael's solid cock pressed against me. Talk about waking up the right way. Boy, am I glad I'm on contraception, there was not a condom in sight last night.

God, I've missed him so. Last night had been a true awakening, for me anyway. This is where we belong -

together. We've been missing out all these years but I'm more than ready to make that time up.

I blink my eyes a few times before looking for what startled my slumber in the first place. My gaze finally lands on Michael, he's seated on the very edge of the bed with his back to me.

I haven't alerted him that I'm awake yet, so I just sit and watch as he rakes his hands through his hair. His shoulders are tensed, almost bunched up around to his ears. I don't want to be the first one to break this weighted silence that we're in. For one, I don't know what the fuck to say after last night. I'm not even fully awake yet and I can already feel the elephant staring at me from the corner of the room.

Was last night a mistake? I honestly hadn't thought so. But what if he did? Everything I was thinking mere seconds ago colors my cheeks with embarrassment.

I guess this is what an out-of-body experience feels like. I've never had one before but as I watch Michael turn around my heart sinks. No, it doesn't sink. It bottoms out, it's probably fallen through the floor and landed right in the kitchen sink.

His eyes look so wild, like he's in pain but I know he's not physically hurt.

I hadn't thought much about the aftermath of last night, I was too busy relishing in it. But least of all, I hadn't been thinking this was a negative thing. Last night had been hot and passionate but most of all it had left me feeling hopeful. We might not get back together straight away but I saw it as a small step in that direction.

Michael's eyebrows furrow together and I have an instinctual feeling I don't want to know what he's thinking because whatever it is, it can't be good.

After a good minute of eye contact, Michael stands and scrambles around to find his clothes. It doesn't take long, he only had a few articles of clothing. Me on the other hand, my clothes may be lost forever. We were in such a flurry last night that it was mostly my six billion layers that went flying, or got shredded at the hands of Michael.

"I can't do this, El." He breathes out as he zips the fly on his jeans.

His eyes are everywhere but on me, maybe that's a small mercy on my part. I can't stand the thought of him watching me as I break down.

I clench my lips together to keep them from quivering. I keep my eyes trained on the television that hangs on the wall opposite my bed, out of the corner of my eye I see Michael pull on his t-shirt.

"Last night was a mistake. We've been down this road before, and I can't handle the fallout again. It's not worth it." His voice is strong, his meaning ringing loud and clear.

"Just go." My voice almost sounds like a whisper but it's early, the house is eerily quiet, there's no way he didn't hear it. It takes a second for my words to spur him into action. He closes my door behind him, finally allowing me to breathe again.

It's not worth it. He means I'm not worth it.

One part of me is absolutely raging. I'm worth

fucking E-V-E-R-Y-T-H-I-N-G. He'd be lucky if I were to want him back. I damn well know what I'm worth.

But then there's another part of me, a part that is crushed. Because he's right. What I put him through eight years ago nearly broke me for good. I had my reasons and I still stand by my decision today but I would never wish that pain on anyone. I've hated myself every day since for putting him through that but there's nothing I can do to make this all easier on him.

Deep down I know that break up scarred him, it's why I understand where he's coming from. He's only trying to protect himself. But I hate that it's from me, it tears me apart inside. A gut-wrenching ache that won't go away because I'm the thing he's most afraid of. Not his job as an F.B.I agent, not bullets flying towards him, not even global warming - the Earth's sign that the planet is dying. Me.

I held power over his heart once upon a time, and I broke it.

It was crazy for me to think we could go back to the way we once were. We're older, different than who we used to be. Just because we were in love once doesn't mean we can be that way again.

I'm just glad I hadn't told him about the baby. I was going to. I was going to explain the other half of the story, a side that I know for sure he hasn't heard yet. He may not hate me anymore, we did manage to clear that up yesterday but here I was hoping for more. That maybe after I told him it wasn't just us I had been thinking of, he'd come around to trusting me again.

I didn't want to hurt him back then, I don't plan on hurting either of us ever again. Not like that.

I pull myself from the bed intending to get ready for the shitty day ahead. And, *fuck! My car!* I suppose I had better put my sneakers on. How else is a shitty day expected to start if not with a 3-mile walk? I'm sure my boss won't mind if I show up to work tired and sweaty. I cringe inwardly and hop to it.

CHAPTER EIGHT

"HAVE YOU SEEN ELLIE?" My mom hedges nonchalantly. I know deep down she's burning with curiosity though. From the very beginning, she was taken with El.

We've just sat down for dinner. It's always been a household tradition that Friday night is pizza night. Meaning, despite the endless amount of tubs currently sitting in momma's fridge freezer, I went to pick up our favorite pizzas from the local Pizza Hut. I'm in my mid-twenties, I know what most would say about this situation. Hell, I know what my friends say, I know how very different their relationships are with their parents. But to me being close with my mom is the most natural thing in the world.

I'm not one bit surprised when Mom mentions El, I knew this would bring up some old memories for her. The last Friday night I spent in this house was only a week after Ellie and I broke up. It was tough, I was beside myself. Momma tried so hard to make me feel better about the whole situation but in the end, I got angry at her too.

She told me it would be alright, that everything would work itself out. I didn't believe her. Little does she know, that even now, things aren't alright. Everything is even more fucked up than before.

That Friday night I locked myself in my room, I ignored her, I screamed. I said some hurtful things. The next morning when I'd calmed down from our fight, I apologized. I still didn't believe that everything would be okay but I was about to leave for college, I didn't want to leave on a bad note. Then momma sat me down and she told me the story of her and my father. I'd thought I'd heard the story before but not that version. Safe to say, it tilted my perspective a little bit.

Since my dad left my mom when she was pregnant she never really got the option of having more kids. I wanted her to be happy, so I've always tried to be open to the idea of her dating, even remarrying but it never happened. I hadn't realized just how much she'd wanted more kids until I introduced Ellie as my girlfriend.

"Oh, yeah. I bumped into her a few days ago." Aside from that, I don't know what else there is to say. So as much as I'd love to give mom what she's clearing looking for, I can't.

"You know she's an interior designer now?" No, I hadn't known that. I have often wondered what Ellie ended up doing with her life.

"Yep, she's a smart girl that one got a job here in

town right out of college." I can say, at the very least, that I knew she worked in town but that's it. I hadn't exactly taken the time to talk to El yesterday. Of course, after this morning I doubt she'll ever say more than 'fuck you' to me again.

Mom continues talking, eventually moving topic to the neighbor's kids that are off to college this year. I chuckle when she says she won't miss them, 'with all their loud no-word music and their sex parties during the day when they think no one's around'. *I fucking love my mom.*

Somehow she always seems to have the funniest stories to tell, and the way she tells them warms my heart. It's an easy decision to tell her about the promotion at work, about the big move. No matter where I live and how many memories I have to drive past every day, I know it'll be worth it.

"I have some big news." I stop eating and drop my fork, when she hugs me I'd rather not be holding a sharp utensil. "I got a promotion at work. They're transferring me to the Lisle field office, which means I'll be moving back home."

"Aw, congratulations Michael, that's the best news!" She lets out a squeal as she pushes away from the table and throws herself at me.

"I was going to wait until I started but I couldn't keep you hanging that long." I just knew she'd be thrilled. I smile as happiness crinkles the corners of her eyes.

"So, when did all this happen? How long do you have left up in Connecticut?" She settles herself back in her seat but all her attention is ever so clearly on me.

"I got the news that there was a position over this way, I went for it and I got told to pack my things a few days later. I put in the rest of my vacation days so that I'd have plenty of time to find a place before I had everything shipped." I still haven't packed up my apartment up in Connecticut, I was too excited that this was all actually happening. I hadn't even thought about how moving home would actually make me feel, until the first time I pulled into mom's driveway. It all hit me very hard, and suddenly, as momma came rushing out the door.

"You've made me so happy! My son is finally coming home." She squeezes me once more before letting go and reclaiming her seat at the dinner table. "And you're sure this has nothing to do with a certain brunette?"

"No mom. I mean I like the weather lady and all, but she's a bit out of my age range."

"Funny, you know that's not who I meant," she chastises as she carries her empty plate into the kitchen. Thankfully she drops the conversation favoring to call all my relatives and tell them the good news.

I pull out my phone to check the time. I've still got some time before the taxi gets here. I told the guys to just pick me up from here. It's Friday night, Simon's bachelor party and I'm so pumped that I could honestly use a nap. Or maybe it's all the stress that's worn me out.

I enter the kitchen, plate in hand, and start working on the mountain of dishes stacked up next to the sink. Mom's still bustling around the kitchen, phone tucked between her shoulder and ear as she starts pulling out her Tupperware containers. The woman will have a full fridge and freezer for weeks. I suppose it's only my duty to help her by taking some of the leftovers back to Lynch's with me tomorrow.

At the very least I'll be well fed when I move back to Aurora.

I'm elbow-deep in a dishpan of water when a car honks outside. One look at the clock and I'm pissed, the fuckers are early. I turn and dry myself off before looking apologetically at mom, 'I've got to go," I mouth.

"Hang on Sheryl," she pecks my cheek and waves me off before returning to her conversation with my aunt. I chuckle as she waves goodbye like she's sending me off to preschool. If only she knew I was going out to watch women strip and swing around on a pole.

Before I'm even out of the kitchen another honk sounds from outside. *Fucking pricks.*

Oh, my payback will be sweet. I can't wait for Lynch's family to come around for lunch tomorrow - after they've been to church. I'm sure we'll just have so much to catch up on.

I jump in the back of the cab, the guys are hooting and hollering obnoxiously. I can smell the alcohol on them already. Maybe that's what I need. I'm not a drinker, I never have been but I suppose if you've gotta start somewhere where's better than a strip club? After this week, I need to ease my troubles and push all my incessant thoughts away.

CHAPTER NINE

Ellie

"What the fuck! Ellie?" Evan exclaims. I hadn't even heard him come in, that's how wrapped up I'd been in my meltdown. To be fair, I hadn't expected him home for at least another hour. He must have got off work early.

I really don't know how I got in this position to begin with. I got home from work, plopped myself on the couch and started to break down. I think it's mainly due to the stress of having so many emotions flying around at once. It's been a long hard week and it seems that everything that's been building up has bubbled to the surface. Sometimes a good cry is all you need, it's essentially a stress reliever.

"What's happened now?" he asks once my sobs have somewhat quietened. He rounds the sofa to stand in front of me, I can only see the blur of him but I know without a doubt that his face is twisted.

I push him away as I stand up, I need to escape. If he's going to be arsy with me, he can fuck off too. God! I don't break down that fucking much. "Really? *What's happened now?* If you don't care, don't ask in the fucking first place!" I shout as I storm off.

"I'm sorry. You know that's not how I meant it." He reaches for me and drags me back into his arms. "I hate that you're upset. I've heard you crying in your room. You can turn the telly up as loud as you want Ellie, it won't ever be enough to drown out the sounds of my sister crying," he tells me lovingly as he strokes my hair.

He pulls back to look me in the eye. He's all blurry from the tears but I can still see the concern etched onto his face.

"Talk to me," he begs giving me a slight shake of the shoulders.

"I can't, there's nothing to talk about." My voice breaks as I plead him to drop it. There's so many things making me feel like a bag of shit and they all seem to circle back to Michael. For Evan to understand fully what I'm going through he'd have to know the whole story and the fact is he doesn't know. If I told him now, he'd hate me forever. He'd hate me for keeping all my secrets to myself, for not trusting him enough to let him in.

"Ellie, I can't fix the problem if you don't confide in me," he says. It hurts because I know he means well.

I shake my head, the tears suddenly halted - scared to fall. I back away, wanting the comfort of a closed door between us. "I'll be fine. I just need some time is all," I lie but try to steady a smile to cover it up.

"You're lying. Why are you lying to me? Dammit El, tell me the fucking truth for once," he yells at me. I press my back further into my door glad to have the support. I've only ever seen Evan this mad a few times before. It scared me then and it's scaring me now.

I watch with wide eyes as he picks up the empty vase from the oak sideboard and hurls it at the fridge. I'm not sure what he was aiming for but the vase smashes on impact. Glass shards fly all over the kitchen. I start to get the feeling that not all of this anger is directed towards me. But, the only other person who has this much effect on Evan is Katie and she hasn't been around lat-

Ah.

So maybe all this time when he was asking me what was wrong he wasn't really asking me but taking out his frustrations instead. Evans heavy breathing makes me look up from the kitchen floor. He's stood in place, staring at the mess he's created. His shoulders rise and fall quickly and I suddenly feel sorry for him. He's in pain.

Evan's always been so selfless and carefree. He doesn't ever worry for himself, he always puts everyone before himself. All my life he's been by my side as my protector, my knight in shining armor. I've always come first, to the point where it's frustrated me on occasion. I hate that my big brothers never had anyone to take care of him.

When we met Katie, I saw the sparkle in his eye. For him to explode like this it has to be to do with her but I can't fathom what. Evan may have been taken with

Katie the first moment they met but she wasn't far behind. While they've always had that connection they've never made anything official.

"Evan."

"Yeah?" His shoulders sag, his voice is strained.

I don't know what to say yet. If I ask if he's alright, he's going to say 'he's fine'. If I ask what happened between him and Katie, he's going to say 'nothing'. I don't know how to help him unless he talks to me. I feel my tear ducts opening up, my eyes beginning to mist. My eyes close, my whole body starts to shake.

I don't know if I've ever been so nervous in my whole life.

"I had an abortion." My voice cracks but it works because Evan finally turns around to face me.

The silence is my only response. It's the best response I could have hoped for, really. Means this could all just be a dream, that this whole conversation was make-believe. Maybe it's my sub-conscience bursting with the guilt of keeping this secret from my brother, my best friend.

Evans arms wrap around me, pulling me away from the door. The smell of my brother draws me in giving me comfort. I clutch at his t-shirt as I start crying all over again.

I can't pinpoint the exact reason I'm crying and that only makes me cry harder out of frustration.

I feel guilt for not telling my brother about the abortion when it happened.

I feel like a shit sister for not noticing sooner that Katie had stopped coming around.

I feel a looming sense of loss over my unborn child.

I've kept this bottled up for so long, it brings me relief to know that I don't have to hide it from Evan anymore.

Our family had always been strongly against abortion, there's no way I could've told them. I understand their reasons, they're all pretty valid. It's horrid and cruel. I'd never even thought about it before until I was faced with those two pink lines. At the time, knowing I was going to break up with Michael so he could leave freely, I couldn't bring myself to keep it.

I wanted it. I wanted that life, Michael and I had had it all planned out. Marriage, a bunch of kids, a house with that white picket fence. But then he got that damn acceptance letter to Princeton. His face lit up like a Christmas tree, it was his dream - to be a Princeton man just like his Grandfather. My heart stopped because I knew I wouldn't even be able to talk to him about it.

"When?" Evan croaks, my eyes flicker up to see that his cheeks are wet.

"A long time ago. It was when we were in high school." My shoulders relax as I let out the breath I've been holding. Another reason I've avoiding telling anyone about this is because it's painful to talk about.

Evan's face tightens again, "Did he force it on you?"

If it were anyone else saying that, that could've been taken wildly out of context. Luckily I know my brother like I know my own reflection. "No."

I let go of Evan, once again, to make my way over to the couch. It's been a long day and it's not even over yet.

I feel there's more Evan has to say so I wave him over and start to make myself comfortable against the red leather.

"I didn't tell Michael. I've never told anyone," I tell him.

"I wish you had told me. You know I'd never judge you," he tells me honestly.

"I know that now, but I didn't back then - I was scared," I admit. The weight of being a scared teenager kept me restricted.

"I hate that you went through that alone while I was prancing around raving about football tryouts." I can't help but chuckle lightly. It was only a few days after I went to the clinic that Evan had in fact pranced around raving about making kicker. I think I'll keep that bit of information to myself though, I don't want him feeling any worse about something that was in no way his fault.

"I can't even imagine..." he reaches for my hand, squeezing it tight. I let him squeeze as tight as he needs to, god knows my heart is doing the same thing. "God. I can't believe I didn't know. El, I'm so sorry I wasn't there to support you."

Little does he know.

"You were, actually. It was right about the time that I broke up with Michael," I tell him. It's almost fascinating to watch as his mind connects the dots. In truth, I never really told him what happened between Michael and I. It was just a case of 'we broke up' and 'it's just not going to work out'.

"Was that why you broke up with him?" His inquisitive gaze turns directly to me.

"No. But the reasons I broke up with him are the same reasons why I... didn't keep the baby," I say sighing loudly.

He nods thoughtfully. "I never really thanked you for taking care of me that summer before our senior year. You have no idea how much that meant to me. You didn't know about the baby but you didn't need to, you were still there for me," I tell him.

"They were some rough couple of months. It killed me inside that I couldn't do anything more to help you," he admits.

"I know, but you did enough." I pull him into a hug and slump against him. He's the best twin brother a girl could ask for and I can't express that enough.

"Don't ever feel like you need to keep anything like that to yourself again. I'm here for you. Always." He speaks softly, stroking my hair.

Hmm. And there's my turning point. I start to see a hint of light at the end of the very dark tunnel we've been in for the past hour. I pull back as my thinking hat goes on.

"I hope you know that the same goes," I point back & forth between us. "Whatever's happened between you and Katie, it'll work itself out. The love you guys have runs deep, it'll withstand this."

Evan smiles a small smile at my attempt to try and comfort him. I stand from the couch suddenly exhausted. I pat his shoulder as I pass him by, "You know where I am if you want to talk."

I enter my room and fling myself on my mattress. I can't be bothered changing my clothes so I kick off my shoes and try to relax into the softness of my comforter. The clock on my bedside table reads close to 6:00PM, I haven't even had dinner yet but I don't have the energy to care. Most likely, I'll wake up in the middle of the night, starving, and go on the hunt for food.

After the last hour, I barely remember that this time last night I was in Michael's arms. It feels like a distant memory, if it was even real at all.

With my eyes closed, I can hear the soft voices from the T.V. out in the living room, I let it softly lull me to sleep.

DARKNESS HAS TAKEN over my bedroom but sound fills it. My ringtone that jarred me from sleep. My arms flail around wildly, searching for my phone before it wakes up my brother.

I reach under my pillow to find it hidden and about to go over the side of the bed. I have to squint when I bring the phone up to my face, the brightness burns my retinas. 'Unknown' flashes on the top of the screen, above that it reads that it's 1:17AM. Who the fuck is calling me at one am?

No one I wanna fucking speak to that's for sure.

I press decline but immediately question it, what if the call had been important? Oh well, if it's important I'm sure they'll call back.

I drop my phone back down beside me and settle in

to try and resume my peaceful sleep. Maybe everyone should cry before they go to sleep, it's seemed to work wonders for me.

Or maybe not, as my phone blares out yet again alerting me of yet another phone call. 'Unknown' flashes on the screen again but this time I angrily swipe at it. "Who is this?"

"Hi. Uh, it's Lynch," states the voice on the other end.

"Riiiiiight. Lynch, why the hell are you phoning me?" I growl.

"This is Ellie, isn't it?" he asks me.

"Yeah." I feel my eyes narrow suspiciously, he knows my name.

"I'm sorry, it might clear things up if I mention I'm a friend of Michael Sanderson's," he says.

Oh, shit. "Is he okay?" My mind runs wild with what could've possibly constituted this phone call.

"Oh, yeah. Sorry, I didn't mean to scare you. I just, I think I need your help. I know it's late but I think you should come get Michael." He sounds worried.

"Why?" I inquire.

"He's drunk and... yeah, you'll see when you get here," he tells me mysteriously.

I haven't even agreed and I'm already sitting up and reaching for my converse sneakers I kicked off earlier. "Are you with him?" I ask.

"Yeah," he answers.

"Ok, where are you guys?" I sigh resolutely.

"Martina's Gentleman's Club." I freeze. *HE'S AT A STRIP JOINT!*

"Ellie?" Lynch questions. I must have been silent for too long.

"Stay where you are, I'm on my way." To come and tear Michael a new one, that is. Before he even has a chance to answer I've hung up and am strolling through the living room.

The T.V. is still on and as I peek over the couch I see that my brother's fallen asleep on the couch. I'll wake him up when I get back. I continue downstairs and out the door. After locking up I keep my keys at the ready as I make my way towards the car. The street looks clear but it's dark and there's lots of places for people to hide. Not only have I got my rape whistle attached to my keys but also my car key may seem blunt but it'd be sharp enough to fucking stab an attacker.

Plus, no one wants to be one of those girls from the horror movies. The ones where they finally get to safety but then they can't find the key and end up just wasting time fiddling to unlock the door.

Nope, not me. I am at the ready. Of course, I don't have the pressure of a zombie trying to eat me.

CHAPTER TEN

Michael

MY EYES ROAM AIMLESSLY. I don't want to be here. I don't know what I want anymore. Up until now, I had thought I hated Ellie, but then last night... it was so fucking good. I've never felt so riled up, or so free. Sex with Ellie was always good but that was back in high school, anything she did to me back then was mind-blowing.

But it's crazy how much she's changed while still looking the same, it's like an illusion. Her body is even more gorgeous than before, her racetrack curves only add to her femininity. Back in high school, she was 'hot' or 'sexy', last night she was a fucking goddess. Literally.

But I've got to push last night away from my mind, it'll never happen again. I was trying to push her away this morning but the second those words left my mouth I regretted it. I was acting out of fear and in the process, I've hurt Ellie. I know I have, I saw the look on her face.

After that, I'd be a lucky bastard if she ever spoke to me again.

Maybe that's for the best. That's what I'd wanted in the first place. If she doesn't talk to me then she can't hurt me. She's an enchantress and I need not to be under her spell, no matter how addicted I am to her wickedness.

If only my heart would listen, it continues to pound rapidly in my chest at the very thought of her.

I watch as Davey gets yet another lap dance, the guys all hoot and holler around him. Simon, the groom - the guy this party is actually for, sits at the bar with a beer and a basket of fries. It seems like he's had a good time but it's getting late and for the past half an hour I've been watching as he not so slyly checks his phone, repeatedly.

Scantily clad waitresses hover around, some travelling back and forth from the bar. The place is hopping now, filled mostly with men. A strip club is so not my idea of a good time, I'll have to make a mental note to not let my future groomsmen drag me to a place like this. My eyes are wandering back to the center stage where the main performance is, and that's when it happens. My heart stops.

Standing across the room, the beads parted like curtains around her, is Ellie. Her eyes are already trained on me but I don't like it. I could always read her facial expression so easily. Right now, I hate that I can't tell what she's thinking.

Fuck!

Is she a figment of my imagination? That seems to

be the only logical explanation my brain can come up with. It's the only one that makes sense, especially with the amount of beers I've had to back it up, the theory. *Great, now it's not even physically possible to get away from her. She's attached to my mind.*

She moves from the doorway, expertly dodging between the club patrons and the waitresses. She stops in front of my table, only then do I know that yeah this beauty standing less than three feet away is actually Ellie - the real-life version. And yes, she really is standing right in front of me, in a female strip club. What. The. Fuck.

"You work here or something?" Her eyes flash and I subtly turn my head back to the stage while sipping my whiskey.

Very clearly not the right thing to say, but in fairness, I didn't mean to say that out loud. It was only supposed to be a sarcastic inner comment to distract me from the disappointment in her eyes. I can see it now that she's up close. I'm not man enough right now to look at her again, I can already feel the anger rolling off of her in waves.

"What are you doing here El?" I ask, whilst avoiding her glare. Doesn't exactly seem like her type of place.

"Lynch called me," she answers. That makes my head turn. She rolls her eyes, "said you were drunk and pathetic. I'm here to take you home."

I go to rest my glass back on the small table but she beats me there, picking it up and downing the rest of my whiskey. I'm normally not much of a drinker, I always need to be alert and at the ready for work. This week alone I've probably consumed more alcohol than I did all of last year. I already know that I'm going to be sick tomorrow, I passed that point hours ago so what's the harm in keeping going?

I watch intently, almost transfixed, as her throat bobs as she swallows, the glass pressed to her lips. God, she's such a fucking tease. Making every man in here wish to be that glass.

"Hey, guys. I'm guessing this is the infamous Ellie, it's nice to meet you. Or, should I say, re-meet you. We went to high school together. I'm Lynch." My hardened glare turns on Lynch. I had wondered what he wanted to borrow my phone for before but I didn't want to pry. Fucking idiot, who else would call someone's ex-girlfriend to ask for a lift home from a titty bar.

Lynch must feel the heat of my stare; he scratches at his neck but otherwise keeps completely focused on Ellie.

"Lynch, so you're the guy I should thank for waking me up and dragging me out in the middle of the night? And to a strip joint no less," she snipes. Her hands gravitated to her hips as she was talking but when she's finished she doesn't wait for a response and turns on her heel. "Let's go."

I stand up and hurry after her, mainly because I don't want her being alone here or anywhere in this part of town, especially at this time of night. I shoot Lynch a what-the-fuck look on the way to Ellie's car, he shrugs but we both know he's dead meat in the morning. I jump in the passenger seat of the Prius while Lynch stretches out on the back seat. I make sure

to keep my hands clasped together in my lap to keep
from reaching out and taking Ellie's hand in mine.

I'm thrown back to high school when El was first
learning how to drive. We'd go out to the outskirts of
town, I'd have her in my car practicing to drive. She
used to hate it, always such a nervous little thing. To
keep her calm, I would have to hold her hand over the
gear stick. *I used to love it when she drove.*

The ride back to Lynch's apartment is long and
eerily quiet except for Lynch's directions.

I feel like a dick for making her do this. And for
how I've treated her. I just don't know how I'll be able
to get over our past.

I glance over at El looking for any sign that she'll
forgive me, maybe she'll think this is a funny story that
she can tell her friends. Maybe they'll see right through
it and hate me for messing her around.

All I know for definite is that I need to decide if I
can live without El in my life. And that I'm going to
have a banging headache tomorrow.

CHAPTER ELEVEN

Ellie

I SWING OPEN the front door to tell whoever the hell is ringing the doorbell to knock it off but I'm shocked at the presence in front of me. Fuck, he's still gorgeous. I will admit I might've expected him to show up the day after I dropped him and his buddy home, but when he didn't come I laughed at my own silliness.

"Can I come in?" He squints at me, the afternoon sun shining right in his eyes no doubt.

I step back and let the door fall further open. Michael steps over the threshold and closes the door behind him. I silently lead him into the kitchen where I've been preparing dinner. I resume my station at the chopping board and continue slicing up the vegetables while he stands idly by and watches.

The minutes tick by and so far, I've completely ignored him, but when the silence starts to get boring I look up to see that he's still standing there. I'm curious. "Did you need something?"

It's been a very long day, I can't be bothered with idle chitter chatter. If he's come around here, it's for a reason. I want to know that reason so then I can go about my night like I had planned. A nice hot bubble bath sounds so good, I could melt in a puddle just thinking about it.

"I came to tell you that I'm sorry." His voice is extra gruff which only adds to his sex appeal, but that's not what compels me to turn my head.

He's only been in town about a week and all we've done since then is do this ridiculous dance of hot and cold, on and off. That's not what I wanted. Hell, the only thing I wanted when we first bumped into each other was to be as far away from him as possible.

"You're sorry...?" I don't understand. He has nothing to be sorry for, and everything to be sorry for. I don't know what to do anymore. Does he want me to want him? Does he want me to forgive him and kick him out?

Why does he not look like he's expecting an apology in return? His expression is earnest, almost sad looking.

"My mind has been all over the place this week," he admits openly.

"I did notice," I say nodding my head. I can't help how my lips tip up slightly. Here he is trying to be sincere and I'm just making comments. Well, at least I haven't told him my true feelings about this apology yet, because honestly, it's a bit lacking.

"I don't know what to do whenever I'm around

you," he says, his voice barely a whisper. I watch with weary eyes as he steps around the breakfast bar, his steps are cautious - like there's a tightrope between us and he's testing it.

I turn around to slide the carrots off the chopping board and into the slow cooker. "Well, I don't know what to do with you either. Like what the fuck do you really want from me here, Michael?"

"I'm scared," he says. *Really?* I turn around to find that he's closer, standing exactly where I stood at the bench only moments ago.

"Of what?" I slam the chopping board and knife into the sink before shrugging purposefully at him. "Do you want me to promise that I have no intentions of breaking your heart for a second time within this lifetime? Trust me, I don't want that either."

I release a massive breath. I don't mean to take my anger out on him but I'm frustrated as hell. I don't like feeling like I'm a rag doll, and that's exactly how I've been feeling this past week. And it's not just him, my own mind has been on the brink too, I've also been feeling very wishy-washy about this whole thing.

This time I'm the one to move closer, I rest my hand firmly on his chest needing the connection. My throat goes a little dry as I bring up the unspoken issue. "I had my reasons for breaking us up," I say getting ready to admit the truth.

"I know." He nods.

"No, you don't," I tell him dreading what's to come.

"My mom told me it was for the best. That you were

letting me go because you loved me," he answers pitifully.

"She was right. I wasn't trying to hurt you, that was the last thing I wanted. Walking away from you that day was one of the hardest decisions I've ever had to make. I hated it," I say. I hated not being about to talk to him, to tell him about the baby. But it only would've held him back from his dreams, it would've tied him down - to me. I didn't want to stay knowing he'd rather be elsewhere. All because we got an unlucky condom.

One simple glitch in the systems can change lives. Hell, I've never been able to have sex since. I wouldn't chance it. Accidentally getting knocked up to someone you loved was a completely different ballgame to getting knocked up by a one night stand.

"I loved you so much. Breaking up with you, broke me," he says with a slight hiccup in his voice.

"*Loved*? As in past tense," I ask, dreading the reply.

I smile at his cheekiness. "I will always love you, you know that. So, for the last time, I'm asking you, what you want from me?" I state frustratingly, hating this game of cat and mouse.

"I want all of you," his hand loops around my back and tugs me in closer. I tilt my head back, angling it towards his.

His lips softly brush against mine in an innocent kiss. The longer our lips are connected the hotter I get, there's an inch that gets worse by each passing second. I hear the breathy whisper on my lips as he drags his lips down my jaw to my neck. "Bedroom."

The thought of my brother walking in on us would

not stop me right not but I have a feeling it might put an awkward strain on their relationship.

I walk briskly to my bedroom, bashing the door against the wall as Michael continues to assault my neck. I flip on the light and start to kick off my shoes. He moves his tongue back and forth over my sweet spot and the stickiness between my legs grows damper. My need for him to be down there, between my legs, is making me grow whiny.

Closing the door, Michael throws me onto the bed. "You want it sweet or hard?" He questions as he starts stripping off his clothes.

Hmm. "I want it quick, I have veggies cooking," bursts from my lips.

His lips tilt and his eyes twinkle. He wants to laugh but he's holding back as to not kill the mood. I yank my skirt up and his eyes are quickly transfixed upon the black strip of my thong. He palms his cock over his jeans as I kick off my flats and spread my legs.

"Give it to me. Show me how much you missed me," I urge him on. He quickly strips off his jeans to reveal he's gone commando.

Ooh. I like that. More of that is definitely required in the future. He climbs on the bed and positions himself above me, him between my legs. His hand reaches out to caress my cheek, his lips lock to mine.

"Say it again," he whispers as he begins to light a blazing trail of wet kisses up and down the column of my neck.

"What?" I question him. My mind's gone a complete blank.

"Say what you said before," he demands.

It clicks, I know what he wants me to say but I like this vulnerable side to him. I pretend to think about it but a small nip to my jaw says Michael doesn't like that much.

"You mean... I love you?" I say batting my eyelids up at him.

"Yeah, that. You have no idea how much I love hearing that because I love you too," he growls between kisses.

Michael's tongue invades my mouth as he pushes my thong to the side and slips himself inside. I can feel every muscle in his body tense as he holds himself inside of me, when his pause gets to be too long I clench my inner muscles hoping to spur him on. He pulls out, holding just his tip at my entrance. "Sorry El, getting too caught up in the moment," he apologizes.

"That's nice, but fuck me already," I practically yell at him. He grunts at my vulgar language but starts to move, smooth guided stokes filling me up deliciously with every movement.

"I'm sorry for this past week," Michael whispers in my ear. "I just wish I had been able to come right up to you and whisk you back into my arms, where you belong."

"Well, I'm sorry for breaking your heart eight years ago." It's a heavy apology, we're both silent for a beat after. I can't help but wonder how this is going to work.

He seemed pretty set on us being together, like an

actual couple, but we haven't really talked about how exactly it would work. I roll over while still keeping his arm resting on my waist... and he's fallen asleep. Well, I suppose I have no choice now but to wait until tomorrow. I hope everything goes okay, I don't want anything else to interrupt us from sailing away towards our happily ever after.

EPILOGUE

Michael

"I'm glad you're still here." Ellie's arms wrap around my waist as she sneaks up behind me.

"Just making coffee." I reach for another cup before filling it with the hot brown liquid. I turn around in her arms, wrapping her in mine. "I'm sorry for leaving like I did last time."

"I hated it, but I understand why you did," she says. She smiles a small smile; it's filled with kindness and understanding. I reach up not being about to help it, I graze my thumb over her bottom lip.

"I've missed you." I take my time drinking in her features. I didn't think I'd ever be this close to her ever again.

She presses a kiss to my thumb. "I missed you too." As she speaks her left eyebrow quirks up for a millisecond. It's gone before it's even fully there but I know that twitch well.

"What's on your mind, Ellie?" I ask.

"You know me, I just worry. At least you know that hasn't changed," she says trying to lighten the sudden atmosphere that's descended.

"Tell me. Let me help soothe your worries," I tell her.

"There's just still so much that we don't know about each other, high school was such a long time ago. It's great that the feelings are still there but I worry the more you get to know who I am now you'll be disappointed," she states quietly.

"That could never happen," I tell her with conviction in my voice. How could she ever think that?

I see her eyes flash with something unknown before she breaks eye contact with me.

"Here's an idea, let's get to know each other. What is it that you want to know? I'll tell you anything if you just ask," I say trying to ease her into relaxing so she feels more comfortable to tell me.

"It's more, the other way around. There's something you don't know, something I've wanted to tell you since it happened." She pauses and my mind starts to wander. She's married, she's got children with her ex-husband, she cheated on me in high school...

"What is it?" I ask, rapidly trying to cut off my own thoughts before they start to sink in.

"Well, you know last night how I said you didn't know the real reason...we broke up?" she says shyly.

"Yeah, but I thought we covered that last night?" I answer confused.

"Kind of. Your mom was right in what she said, I

didn't want to hold you back but what I didn't tell you was...," I can see she's visibly struggling to get her words out, instinctually my hands reach for hers. "What you didn't know was that I was pregnant when you left," she finally finishes.

"What?" I answer. My mind unable to comprehend the information that's just been unleashed to me.

"Nearly three months," she adds.

"I don't understand," I say running my hand down my face.

"I had it taken care of after you left. I didn't want to tell you at the time, your life was planned out. I knew what you'd do if I'd told you," she admits. She's visibly shaking.

My resolve weakens. "You still should've told me. El, I deserved to know."

"I know but then you would've wanted to keep it and stay here. I loved you so much I couldn't stand to see you give up your dreams for us. You have to understand, I did what was best for the both of us," she says. Her voice trembles as she speaks.

"I'm sorry El." I feel the tear trail down my cheek, I pull Ellie's body to mine. I squeeze her tight as I continue to leak silent tears. Silently crying over the child I unknowingly lost, over the fact that Ellie went through this all on her own. Over all the time I've spent hating her for causing me so much pain in the past when really it was all my fault.

Ellie's just bared her soul to me, and I vow that she's not going to regret it. I'm going to cherish her for as long as she'll have me because she is worth it. She's worth every bit of heartache I can stand and more. She is my life, the very air I breathe.

"How about we get ready and go out for ice cream?" she says changing the subject and lifting this cloud of sadness that has descended upon us.

"It's not even lunchtime...?" I question her as I try to hold in a bout of laughter.

"I know." She shrugs adorably like that's all the explanation that's required. She turns back around to look me in the eye impatiently awaiting my answer.

My smile grows wide as I shake my head in disbelief. It's not like I'm going to say 'no' to her, is it? I could never, and I would never, say 'no' to her. I just hope she feels the same way.

Tomorrow I plan on sneaking off to see Ellie's parents, I want their blessing because I have a feeling I'm going to be asking Ellie a very important question, and soon. Call me a possessive, insecure beast but I need to know that she's mine. Bonded to me in every way humanly possible. Last time it was so easy for her to walk away, I won't be letting her go again.

The End

AUTHOR'S Note

Dear Readers,

This book was hard to write but for a different reason than I expected. The tale of Michael and Ellie made me really dig deep and pour all of my emotions into each word. I have laughed and I have cried, boy have I cried, while writing this novella - I hope you did too. Next up in the series will be the long-awaited tale of Evan and Katie. This is the one I've been looking forward to, have you noticed all the hints being dropped in the previous books? :P

Thank you ALL so much for sticking with me. I'd like to shout out to my amazingly supportive reader group, my Angels you truly are all ANGELS. To Amanda, I can not thank you enough for all the support and help you've given me. To all my other friends and family, I appreciate the support you've shown as I struggled through.

Thank you for reading Capture Me. I hope you enjoyed this snippet of Ellie & Michael, their story will continue but only as a sideline in the next books. If you did, I welcome you to write a review on Amazon/Goodreads/Bookbub to help promote the book to other curious readers.

And, as always, if you're interested in being kept updated on what I'm working on and my new releases head over to my social media pages or simply email me.

Until next time,

Chelsea xo

OTHER TITLES BY

Chelsea McDonald

The Accord Series:

Lunar Accord, Book 1

Mortal Accord, Book 2 (Coming October 2019)

Vibrations Novella Series:

Save Me

Hold Me

Capture Me

Armstrong Lovers Series:

Claimed (Kennedy & Nathaniel)

The Sapphires Series:

Pretty Little thing, Book 1 (Coming July 2019)

CONTACT THE Author

You can find Chelsea on Facebook:
https://www.facebook.com/AuthorCMcDonald

Instagram:
https://www.instagram.com/AuthorCMcDonald
Twitter:
http://www.twitter.com/AuthorCMcDonald

Or, contact her directly by email:
authorcmcdonald@gmail.com